I0586204

PRANA

A SPIRITUAL FICTION SERIES

WALDMEER SERIES
BOOK 6

DONNA GODDARD

Second Edition 2023

Published by Donna Goddard

Victoria, Australia

Paperback ISBN: 978-0645729658

Large Print ISBN: 978-1764151146

Cover design by Donna Goddard

www.donnagoddard.com

CONTENTS

THE RIGHT HOUSE

SHAMBHAVI

PART III
BORDERFIRMA

NO GOING BACK

GOING BACK

PART IV
MANDALA

MAHASHIVRATRI

EQUINOX

OMNI-ALL

MANDALA'S END

PART I
FOR BETTER OR WORSE

INSPECTION

CHAPTER 1
BETTER OR WORSE

A few months later, in Store Creek:

After six months of living in Store Creek with the cold weather, it was good to finally arrive at spring's doorstep. Merlyn wondered if that was why Ben decided to visit today. He said it was a rental inspection, but that was just a joke. At least, Merlyn hoped it was a joke. Although it had been two years since their separation, they *had* lived together for three years. Nothing needed inspecting.

Merlyn's mind was put at ease once he arrived. He appeared to have no interest in checking on anything. He chatted for an hour or so before saying it was time to return to the city and that he had a big week ahead of him at the State Ballet.

While walking down the dirt driveway, Ben said, "I'm sorry. I know you like living here, but I've decided to sell *Nanna's House.*"

"Oh," said Merlyn as she stopped walking.

That's why he came, she thought.

She knew she had no right to question his decision. She had had the benefit of living in a house she loved with very reasonable rent.

"It's too big an expense," explained Ben. "Holiday houses are a luxury. A luxury I can't afford. You originally said that staying here was only temporary and that you would find somewhere else in Store Creek."

"Yes, of course," said Merlyn.

"I have to do what's best for me," said Ben.

"It's fine," said Merlyn. "You definitely have to do what's best for you."

Ben looked towards the surrounding hills and said, "Marry me."

Merlyn felt she must have misheard him. However, she caught the look in his eyes and knew she had not.

She turned towards the garden in an attempt to order her thoughts. There were many reasons to say *no*. Many more to say, *Let's see.*

She looked closely at the overgrown garden. She never did clean it up as she had promised. It wasn't laziness. She couldn't bring herself to interfere with it. It was doing such a magnificent job on its own. The Carolina jasmine was covered in large, trumpet-type, yellow flowers—toxic to children but too beautiful to remove, with no immediate danger. She could smell its perfume when the breeze came their way. Below the climber, the ground was covered with tiny, blue forget-me-nots that had spread unconfined for the past few decades. Nothing looked stressed or confused or in need of a momentous decision.

For some reason, possibly due to the forget-me-nots, she said just as quietly as Ben had, "Yes."

As he was in no state to hear anything subtle, Ben

continued, "I know it's unexpected, after two years and all. In the beginning, I thought I'd be better off without you."

Although a little offended, Merlyn wanted Ben to finish what he had to say. He may not say these words again.

"The thing is," said Ben. "I'm worse off without you. And even if I wasn't, I don't want to be without you."

He couldn't say any more. That was all he had.

"I already said *yes*," said Merlyn, taking his hand. "Anyway, technically speaking, I said *yes* five years ago, and that still applies because we are still married."

Ben smiled and pulled Merlyn towards him. He was considerably taller than she. She breathed in the smell of his chest. It smelled good. It seemed so long since she had smelled it, yet it was still very familiar.

Pushing aside the overhanging vine from the front door, Ben light-heartedly complained, "I don't know why we have to have a front door that is so well camouflaged that it is a mission to get back into our own home."

CHAPTER 2
TOUCH ME MORE

The next morning, Merlyn heard the early birds chatting amongst themselves. Even they seemed to sense something was different.

She looked at Ben's sleeping body. He was peaceful. She reached over and touched his back lightly enough so that he wouldn't wake. He hated being touched when he was asleep. He found uninvited touching and draped limbs annoying and intrusive. Even when he was awake, he liked to be touched when *he* wanted to be touched. Merlyn thought it was a condition common to male dancers who tire of female advances in an industry that, of necessity, highly values male bodies.

She slipped out from under the bedcovers. They were heavy and warm. Too warm. A sleeping man in the bed generates a lot of heat, and she had to throw off the bulk of them during the night. Normally, she slept with a tonne of them as the nights in Store Creek were very cold. All the cracks in the floorboards and around the windows made the house the same temperature as outside. It was particularly cold on those clear, star-studded nights when the deep, black sky, with its universe of lights, seemed to talk of other worlds much bigger than this one.

Quite a lot later, Ben sat in the small kitchen with its old, yellow cupboards, eating breakfast. He stared out the window.

"I still think we should sell my grandmother's house," said Ben. "I'm too busy with work, and you will be with me in the city. Right?"

"No," said Merlyn.

"No?" asked Ben. "Fine. Then stay in Store Creek on your own."

"I don't want to live in Store Creek," said Merlyn, "but I also don't want to live back in the city."

"Where then?" asked Ben.

"Waldmeer," said Merlyn.

"Waldmeer?" asked Ben. "Why? I mean, it's nice and all, but why?"

"There is something there for me, Ben," said Merlyn.

"What sort of something?" asked Ben suspiciously.

"I don't know what it is, but I know that it's there," said Merlyn. "You sell here. I'll find somewhere to rent in Waldmeer, and you can come to Waldmeer on your days off."

"That's no way to be married," said Ben.

"Maybe not," said Merlyn, "but we have to compromise until we're on the same path."

By now, Ben knew that if he wanted this to work, he had to not insist on his own way. He had already tried that. It led to a total breakdown. This way didn't seem ideal, but at least it was a start. He decided to take it.

Sensing his acceptance, Merlyn reached over and kissed him on the forehead.

He relaxed and looked like he was thinking, *Why don't you touch me more often?*

ESTHER

CHAPTER 3
THE INTRODUCTION

Two weeks later, at the State Ballet:

As Ben walked through the glass doors of the State Ballet building, he came across one of the company's older professionals, who had been a friend for many years.

"Morning," said the man. "How's Store Creek going?"

"Fine," said Ben. "I suppose."

Two weekends had passed since Ben saw Merlyn. He hadn't spoken to her, nor messaged. He kept checking his messages to see if she had messaged, but she hadn't.

Seeing the look on Ben's face, his friend said tentatively, "Look, buddy, I thought you were back together, but if things aren't going quite to plan, I have a suggestion."

He waited to see Ben's reaction. There was no obvious displeasure from Ben about a suggestion, so he continued.

"The missus and I have had our ups and downs over the years. I think most people think that we have been very fortunate with our marriage, and we have been. But everyone has their problems. God knows we've had many."

Ben looked surprised because his friend's marriage was one of the few he had always admired. Becoming more interested, he looked at his friend and indicated to go on.

"A few years back," said the man, "we were having a particularly difficult time, and someone suggested a therapist to us."

At the mention of a therapist, Ben noticeably baulked.

"Before you get all snarky," said the man, "you might want to think about it. She's very good. And close by here."

Patting Ben's arm reassuringly, he said, "You've got nothing to lose by trying it. My guess is that if you don't, you probably have lots to lose."

Ben looked sad, almost defeated.

"Cheer up, buddy," said the man, "Esther, the therapist, says, *We have many relationships, and several of them are with the same person.* I will email her and introduce you. No pressure, but she is busy, and if you want to go, you might have to wait a long time without an introduction."

CHAPTER 4
E. G. PSYCHOLOGY

The next afternoon, Ben stood outside E.G. Psychology. He assumed that E.G. stood for Esther Graham, the name he had been given. The therapist emailed saying an appointment was available today due to a cancellation. Out of desperation, not enthusiasm, he took it.

When Esther came downstairs to open the front door and the black metal gate, Ben couldn't help feeling that he was being led into a fortified prison. He tried to shake off the feeling that he might never get out or that something dreadful might happen to him while he was *inside*.

Esther was an attractive woman in her mid-thirties. That bothered Ben. Not her attractiveness, but her age. He assumed that whoever was capable of helping his friend must have been a more mature person. The last thing he was going to do was open up about his personal life to some relatively new psychologist to make them feel good about their professional abilities.

"I'm Esther," said the woman, beckoning Ben upstairs.

The building was old, but Esther's office had a modern, light, white look.

"I assume you are Benjamin," said Esther.

She reached out her hand in a confident but contained manner.

Ben took it and said, "Ben is fine. Everyone calls me Ben."

Esther did not reply but indicated that Ben should sit wherever he pleased. He chose a comfortable-looking, single-seat lounge chair and glanced around the room. It was tastefully decorated and included a few healthy plants, which broke up the clinical look. The only thing which seemed a little out of place was an impressive painting of a beautiful woman from ages past with long, red, curly hair.

Noticing Ben's glance, Esther said, "She's Esther, the Jewish queen, from the Book of Esther. Her birth name was Hadassah, but later, when she married and became queen of Persia, her birth identity needed to be hidden. So, her name was changed to Esther, which means to hide or conceal."

The significance of that was not lost on Ben.

Taking the opportunity to lighten the conversation, he said warmly, "Is that who your parents named you after?"

"We are here to talk about you now, Benjamin," said Esther.

The whole first session was spent with Esther asking Ben about his life circumstances and relationships, both intimate and otherwise.

"Our time is up for now," said Esther, "but if you would like to return, I have another cancellation this coming Friday."

Ben paid the $180 fee and felt that it was a lot of money to pay someone for telling your life story. He returned the following Friday for his appointment, not out of faith in the process but because he couldn't bear to part with that much money without getting something in return.

CHAPTER 5
LIT UP

Ben got a little more "something" than he had
anticipated.

"It's emotional torture," said Esther in a calm
but definite manner during the early stages of the Friday
session. "It's emotional torture of people who fall in love
with you."

Looking at the wall clock, Ben wondered if he could
leave without paying for today and cut his losses for the first
session. Before he made his move, he composed himself
enough to look at Esther's face. She looked relaxed and intelligent, not the demeanour of someone meaning to offend.

"You don't do it intentionally. Nevertheless, you do it,"
said Esther. "Now, let me explain."

Ben wondered if it was a psychological tactic to insult the
client to get their attention. If so, it was working.

"You have two relationship patterns you oscillate
between. The first goes like this," said Esther. "Over your
forty years, you have had a few genuine love affairs —
people you sincerely fell in love with, and they with you.

Confident people. Talented, as you are. Good matches. But as soon as things got difficult, you deteriorated into fear, blame, and anger instead of dealing with it. They were self-assured enough not to put up with that, and the relationships broke down. Inevitably."

Esther remained silent to let Ben absorb what she was saying. Ben was still stunned, but also still listening.

"The second pattern goes like this. In between each genuine love affair, you make other relationships to recover your sense of control. You choose people who are in love with you, but you are not in love with them. You stay because you can manage it. At some level, you resent both their neediness and yourself for being there. But it feels safer than the pain of something real. For the person in love with you, it's torture. They spend the whole relationship trying to convince themselves that you want them, while you do a thousand small and big things to indicate that you don't. Eventually, you can't stand it anymore. You move on, possibly with regenerated courage for another attempt at a more genuine connection elsewhere."

Again, Esther stopped speaking to let Ben assimilate this information.

"Are you saying I'm a control freak?" ventured Ben.

"Control is a defence mechanism," said Esther.

"Against what?" asked Ben.

"Fear," said Esther. "Fear of being hurt."

After a pause, Esther continued, "I have given you a lot to think about, and I do not expect you to agree with all the information I have given you. I do not want you to agree. Instead, I would like you to think about what I am telling you so that you can understand your behaviour patterns. You don't have to become a therapist (that's for those of us who really enjoy torture), but you do need to understand yourself better if you wish to be happy."

Ben wondered if the therapeutic torture bit was a joke, although Esther wasn't smiling.

"Understanding ourselves takes work and courage," said Esther. "Whether or not we choose to do it is up to us. Although, essentially, we don't have a choice because, eventually, the pain will make it intolerable. It's more a matter of how much pain we are willing to endure before we undergo the 'pain' of transformation. At least, the latter pain gets us somewhere."

Esther looked at the large clock on the wall, although it wasn't necessary because her sense of timing was impeccable.

"Our time is up for today," she said. "Let me leave you with a quote about fear and change from one of my teachers-in-spirit, the existential philosopher Soren Kierkegaard. He said, *Whoever has learned to be anxious in the right way has learned the ultimate.* Or, in popular vernacular, we could say, *Feel the fear and do it anyway.*"

As Ben walked past the print of Queen Esther, he wondered if she might not be a little less intimidating than Esther of E.G. Psychology.

It would be an even match, he thought.

He descended the stairs from that peculiar room, a mix of learned academia, incomprehensible philosophers, mystic queens of centuries passed, soul-searching, and confrontation. It was not a place he liked to be. Nevertheless, as the heavy gate closed after him, he noticed that, along with the shell shock, something new and unfamiliar seemed to have lit up inside himself.

YIN AND YANG

CHAPTER 6
GOOD THINGS

"You don't have to come," said Ben on the phone.

"I'll come," said Merlyn. "I'm pleased that you are seeing someone. I just didn't know."

"She's a shrink," said Ben. "Not a date."

Merlyn ignored that comment.

"She sent my next appointment time," said Ben, "and suggested I bring you because 'the therapeutic process can then be applied to current relationship issues.' Her words. Not mine."

Both Merlyn and Ben were silent at the prospect of what that might mean. Feeling that the heat of the sessions could be partially diverted onto someone else, Ben was more in favour of couple therapy than he would have imagined. He secretly hoped that Esther would find things in Merlyn that he could not articulate.

"You said she's younger than us," said Merlyn.

"Yes," said Ben, "but don't let that put you off. She's easy to talk to. The whole thing is easy."

Ben felt the lie of that bubble up through his stomach.

In Esther's psychology room:

The one-hour counselling session went by very smoothly and rather pleasantly. For some reason, Esther approached this session in an entirely different manner. Towards the end, she asked them both to say three good things they honestly valued about the other person.

"You first, Ben," said Esther.

"Okay," said Ben, gathering his thoughts. "You are kind. "

Merlyn smiled appreciatively.

"You are smart," he continued.

Merlyn raised her eyebrows.

"I mean," said Ben, "you're not smart like Esther."

Merlyn lowered one eyebrow and moved her mouth sideways.

"Because Esther is very educated," said Ben.

Feeling that the conversation needed to be redirected, Ben added, "You are smart in yourself, Merlyn."

Merlyn accepted that.

Esther urged Ben on, "And one more thing."

Ben became quiet and said, "You love me."

"And you, Merlyn?" said Esther.

"You are funny," said Merlyn. "You make me laugh."

Ben smiled.

"You are handsome," said Merlyn.

Ben straightened his posture.

"Actually, it's not so much that," said Merlyn introspectively.

Ben frowned.

"It's that you are handsome to *me*," said Merlyn.

Ben frowned more.

Esther intervened in a matter-of-fact way and said, "Beauty is in the eye of the beholder."

"I know good-looking women," said Merlyn, following that train of thought, "who are not good inside and...."

Deciding to abandon that conversation, Ben said, "One more thing, Merlyn."

"You are a wonderful dancer," said Merlyn as if that would, obviously, be at the top of anyone's list.

Ending the session, Esther said, "That's enough of a good thing for now."

CHAPTER 7
GOOD POINTS

"Are you staying?" asked Ben as they left E.G. Psychology and walked the few streets back to the State Ballet.

"I can't," said Merlyn. "We haven't had a chance to talk lately, but I have things to tell you."

A chance to talk was used very loosely.

"Yes?" said Ben.

"I found somewhere to rent in Waldmeer," said Merlyn. "Actually, I didn't find it. Malik from Waldmeer Warriors did. I told him I was looking for somewhere when I was last there. There are no long-term rentals available in Waldmeer, only holiday houses, and they are way too expensive. I thought Malik might hear of something available to local people. He said the family across the road from him had an empty granny flat because the old lady who lived there recently died. When he asked the owners, they were reluctant but said yes on one condition."

"What's the condition?" asked Ben.

"The lady had an old dog," said Merlyn. "It comes with the flat. It's a Cavalier King Charles Spaniel."

"A what?" asked Ben.

"You know," said Merlyn, "a Cavalier. Those little brown and white dogs with long ears. They're not the smartest dog in the world, but they love everyone and are very gentle. Her name is Bella."

Ben didn't look like he cared what her name was. He didn't want a dog. He certainly didn't want an old, dumb dog.

"You know I don't want a dog," said Ben. "I thought we were supposed to be working together. And I don't want a tiny flat on someone else's property."

Merlyn knew that Ben had a point...or two.

"There isn't anything else available," she said. "I need to be in Waldmeer. It's important. To me."

After a pause, she added, "And Bella was pleading with me to take her."

Seeing the emotion in Merlyn's eyes, Ben groaned.

"Can you please give it a try?" said Merlyn. "If it doesn't work, we will think of something else."

Ben wasn't so sure that she would think of something else or that there was *something else* to be thought of.

"I'll come this weekend," sighed Ben. "Anyway, I have an offer on Store Creek, and I need to stop there on the way to you."

CHAPTER 8
IN HEAVEN AND ON EARTH

I*n Waldmeer:*

When Merlyn arrived back in Waldmeer late that afternoon, she let Bella out, fed her, and continued with the task of cleaning the granny flat.

Although most of the old lady's things had been thrown out, some memorabilia were still scattered between the few rooms. They were mostly dog-related. A mug that said something about dogs loving us more than we love ourselves. An old-fashioned picture of various dog breeds that said if Heaven didn't have dogs, then the preferable place would be wherever the dogs were. Merlyn hoped that wherever the lady was, there were dogs.

"You probably miss her," said Merlyn as she patted Bella on the head. "Never mind, I'll look after you."

Bella didn't look particularly sad. For all their love, Cavaliers are accept-the-moment-as-it-is type dogs. Given an open door or a hole in the fence, Cavaliers will happily trot off, blissfully unaware of danger, trusting that the world is merely waiting for their smiling appearance.

On the opposite end of the scale are German shepherds. Ever alert for the slightest trouble, they are not at all trusting that the world is fine. Errant open doors and fence holes are cause for stress, not for happy adventuring. And therein lay a problem. Bella was not the only dog that the lady owned. She had a German shepherd brother, Albert (or Bertie as the lady was fond of calling him). The flat owners had given him to the Waldmeer car yard to use as a guard dog.

Although Albert was a senior citizen, he still had the German shepherd fire. He was capable of guarding, but he did not consider the car yard his to guard. At every opportunity, he escaped the yard and found his way back to the granny flat. He would lie at the door, waiting patiently for his mistress to return. He could not accept that she was not coming back. German shepherds get heartbroken about things like that. Each time, the car yard owner came to fetch him.

That evening, Merlyn settled into her snug bed and looked at Bella, already asleep on the mat. She was fairly sure the lady let Bella sleep on the bed, but Merlyn was strict about that.

"Beds are for humans only," she would scold at the bottomless, brown eyes.

On hearing muffled scuffling outside, Merlyn hesitantly opened the front door to a large dog. She assumed it was the German shepherd that had lived there. Albert looked at her cautiously, as if deciding something. Dogs decide things quickly and instinctively. They rarely change their minds.

He relaxed his ears, put his head down, and went inside. He was big for a little place, but was accustomed to manoeuvring his Heffalump body in and around the tight space. Bella's arthritis prevented her from easily jumping up to greet Albert. Heading straight for her, he curled around Bella so that they made a circle like Yin and Yang.

Albert stared at Merlyn, breathed out, closed his eyes, and went into a deep sleep.

He was home.

He knew it. Bella knew it. Merlyn knew it.

It was only Ben who was yet to find out.

PART II
PRANA COMMUNITY

COMMUNITY

CHAPTER 9
MIXED DRINKS

"Weak latte (no sugar). Hot chocolate," yelled the Waldmeer barista.

Merlyn grabbed her coffee and headed for the door.

They put sugar in my coffee, she thought as she sipped it. *Hang on, that's not sweet coffee. It's hot chocolate. The orders have been muddled. Oh, well, it tastes delicious.*

She then turned her thoughts to the recipient of her latte, who would be missing their order of hot chocolate. Looking around for a likely suspect, she easily spotted a woman about her age staring at her drink. Merlyn wondered what her reaction would be. The woman seemed to be weighing up the benefits of caffeine versus sugar and, like Merlyn, decided to go with the flow. Merlyn then realised that the mixed-drink recipient was Esther, the psychologist.

"Hello," said Merlyn. "What a surprise to see you in Waldmeer."

"Hi," said Esther.

Mentally running through a checklist of her clients' names, Esther added, "Merlyn."

"Do you have clients in town?" asked Merlyn, who then realised the question was overstepping a professional line.

Esther was adept at such things. She pointed to the brilliant ocean and said, "You are lucky to live here."

"Yes, it's beautiful," said Merlyn. "I moved here not long ago."

She was going to say something about Ben, but felt like it would be *speaking out of school.*

After a moment of quiet, Esther said, "I'm on my way to Prana Community in the Leleks. I often go there. It's about an hour and a half from here, through the forest, and then winding back to the coast."

She nodded in the direction of the faraway coastline.

"Really?" said Merlyn. "I have never heard of Prana Community."

"It's a spiritual group," said Esther, "founded a few decades ago by Bob Owens. I've only been involved for the past few years, after Bob's time. He adopted the yogic path after being healed of an illness. I'm Jewish, but Bob never minded where people came from or what they went back to."

"Who runs Prana Community now?" asked Merlyn.

"Some of his loyal students and friends," said Esther. "The main intake person is a woman named Verloren. She told me that she had a holiday house in Waldmeer years ago, but that she rarely comes here nowadays. I always drive through Waldmeer because I love the ocean views. She drives through the back hills because it's quicker. If it weren't for her, the place would have gone bankrupt after Bob died.

She stepped in, sorted it out, and has been doing so ever since."

"Can I visit Prana Community?" asked Merlyn.

"You can come with me," said Esther. "There is one problem."

"Yes?" asked Merlyn.

"It would mean you cannot come to me as a counselling client again," said Esther.

"Could Ben still see you on his own?" asked Merlyn.

"Sure," said Esther.

"So long as he can still see you," said Merlyn. "Anyway, I'd much prefer gurus to psychologists and yoga communities to counselling offices."

CHAPTER 10
CLIFF HANGER

I n *Prana Community:*
The wooden sign at the entrance of Prana Community read,

This land is our mother.
Its water, our blood.
Its dirt, our bones.
The sunrise, our hope.
The sunset, our peace.
Come to learn.
Leave to practise.

Esther scanned the virgin forest of giant gums and luscious ferns and said, "It was important to Bob that people learned to live without harming the land. Even now, the community has no town utilities—water, sewerage, and electricity. In the early days, they relied on generators for lighting and power. However, the generators were noisy and caused pollution. So, Bob invented a mini hydropower plant on the river. It's simple but works well and makes enough clean, quiet electricity to keep the community out of the dark."

"Who lives here?" asked Merlyn.

"There's a small team who have made their lives here," said Esther. "Everyone else travels back and forth from wherever home is. Bob always intended people to go back into the world and take their spiritual practices with them."

"Welcome," said a woman walking up to the car.

She looked in her early seventies and was well dressed, particularly for a forest.

"I'm Verloren," she said warmly. "We are happy to have you here. Let me run you through some of our community rules. Day visitors are given more freedom than those who stay, but we still request that you hand your phone into the office and, of course, no alcohol or drugs are permitted. Other than that, visitors are free to experience this special place in whatever way feels most comfortable to them. We trust the process. We are here to create a healthy body, a clear mind, balanced emotions, and an aligned energy field."

She paused as the cockatoos and kookaburras squawked and laughed.

"In our teacher's words," said Verloren, "'If you have mastery over your physical body, you have 20% mastery over your life. If you have mastery over your mind, you have 60% mastery over your life. And if you have mastery over your whole energetic being, you have total mastery over your life.'"

Verloren paused again as the birds competed to see who could make the most noise.

"We do not always have control over what happens in the

outside world," continued Verloren, "but we can learn to control what happens on the inside."

After meandering through the array of buildings, Esther and Merlyn wandered along a narrow path towards the ocean. They came to a clearing. Esther stopped talking to let the view speak. On the edge of a cliff was a breathtaking temple.

"It's Ajna Temple," said Esther. "It's our pride and joy, although we're not big fans of pride here. We're only big fans of joy."

She looked with wondrous, appreciative eyes both at the temple and the sea. This was an entirely different Esther from the one Merlyn had seen at E.G. Psychology. In her professional setting, she was intelligent, alert, and polite. However, she was also reserved, impartial, and not really a real person. Here, with the ocean roaring, the wind blasting, the forest calling, and the temple drawing its prey into its sacred centre, Esther was a different creature. More alive, relaxed, and beautiful. A very real person.

Perched on the cliff but not looking in the least vulnerable, Ajna Temple was awe-inspiring. It radiated a tangible and pulsing energy field that was, at the same time, irresistible and a touch frightening. Merlyn wanted to immerse herself in the temple's otherworldly power, but Esther said it was time to return to the community hall for satsang.

CHAPTER 11
IN TIME

L ater that day, when the two women reluctantly got ready to leave, Verloren reappeared and said to Merlyn, "Esther told me that you live in Waldmeer."

"Yes," said Merlyn, giving her street name.

"The house I once owned was a few streets from you," said Verloren. "I originally bought it off my friend, Farkas, and then, after five years, he bought it back off me."

"I know him," said Merlyn. "He runs the dance aerobic classes at the Waldmeer Warriors. I haven't spoken to him much, but I often speak to Ide, his ex-partner and mother of their child Lan-Lan."

Verloren smiled but did not want to be drawn into that conversation.

"Old friends of mine, Lucy and Lenny," said Verloren, "lived directly across the road from you. I knew Lucy when she managed the Waldmeer Corner Store and Cafe."

"I haven't heard of that cafe," said Merlyn.

"No," said Verloren, "it has long since gone, along with

dear Lucy. I also knew Lucy's daughter, Maria. Once, I visited her in Eraldus when she had a spiritual healing practice there."

Verloren momentarily frowned at the memory but seemed to be telling herself something (or someone was telling her), and she shook the feeling off.

∽

INTERLUDE:

When Maria was in her mid-twenties, before Amira took full control of their shared body, she lived in Eraldus and had a healing practice. At that stage, Verloren was highly jealous of her, particularly her relationship with Farkas, for whom Verloren had deep, unrequited feelings. After an unexpected and tense visit to Maria in Eraldus, we were told of Verloren:

> *In time, Verloren would return. Time is not necessary for healing, but it is inevitable. We find many friends when we are down and out. People swarm around with procla-mations of, "Oh, how dreadful. How terrible." They may as well say, "Thank you so much for making me feel better about myself and my life. You have more problems than I and are more pathetic." Yet, when we enter the healing path, few will be standing there to wish us well, in case we find it.*

Indeed, in time, Verloren did return. She returned to herself. She entered the path of healing, and the ones meant for her were standing there beside her.

"When Maria moved back to Waldmeer from Eraldus," said Verloren, "she seemed much older and had changed her name to Amira. At the time, I thought it was a result of her parents' sudden deaths and the strange illness that came over her. Much later, when I started to understand the energetic world, I wondered if something spiritual might have happened to her."

Merlyn and Esther sensed that Verloren needed to tell this story and listened attentively. Besides, it was interesting. The difference between gossip and a healing story is that the latter has no ill will.

"I saw Amira occasionally, but we never spoke much," said Verloren. "I remember helping her, at one stage, by seconding a motion she wanted to get passed for the one-hundredth anniversary of the Convent. She was trying to get a minority group, the Clinkers, represented in the decision-making process."

Verloren smiled and recalled, "It still makes me laugh when I think of the look on her face when she realised that I was the only one in the room willing to support her."

"A few years after that," said Verloren, "when I put my Waldmeer house on the market, I vividly remember Amira stopping outside my house. I can even remember that it was a brilliant blue day. I told her I had been having a recurring dream in which a man kept telling me, *'Don't change your location. Change your approach.'"*

"Amira's son, Malik, lives in her old house with his family," said Merlyn, who was rather pleased to fill in some missing information. "At least, I assume it's the same Amira.

They call her Faith-Amira, but it would surely be the same person."

She remembered the children's names and added, "The youngest daughter is called Maria, apparently after her grandmother."

"That's strange," said Verloren. "I heard that Amira's cousin, Faith, took over that house and that her son and grandchildren live there. Anyway, Amira would not be old enough to have grandchildren that age. And I've never heard a single word about an elusive man being around long enough to father three children to Amira. No, no, she just disappeared."

AJNA AND MANIPURA

CHAPTER 12
CRACKING NUTS

Bob Owens's Indian guru was a tough nut. His students never knew what he was going to do next. He did all manner of things to surprise, awaken, and shake his students from their mindsets. His followers were certainly kept on their toes. He had a relatively small group of followers. Bob was unsure if that was by the Master's choice or if most people couldn't tolerate his style.

Once, the guru sent a letter to Bob, who was living on his coastal land (now Prana Community) in the Leleks. He asked Bob to come immediately to India to see him. Bob had only recently returned home from a trip to his guru. It was a long, expensive, and tiring journey in those days. Nevertheless, he devotedly set off the next day. With plenty of time to ponder what could possibly be so important that the Master would call him again so soon, Bob dared to entertain the possibility that his guru might pass on special secrets of the mystic path.

Maybe, thought Bob, *it is enlightenment.*

Barely containing his excitement when he reached the

Master's house in the South Indian village, Bob thought about how much he loved the Master.

He has given me so much. He has given me a new life and taught me everything I know, at least everything of importance that I know. Yes, it's challenging, but where would I be without him? Lost and going around in pointless circles.

Exhausted but full of love and with tears in his eyes, he opened the door and said, "Master, I have come. I am here. I spared no time or expense in returning as quickly as possible. Tell me, dear teacher, how may I serve you?"

"Why are you here again?" asked the guru with barely a glance towards the door where the dirty, hungry Bob stood expectantly.

Although confused, Bob persevered.

"Master, you sent a letter asking me to come. I came as quickly as possible."

"Oh, yes, so I did," said the Master. "I forgot. Anyway, it mustn't have been important."

With a wave of his hand and a slight chuckle, he dismissed Bob. To say Bob was shocked would be an understatement of grand proportions. He stood motionless. Incredulous.

"But Master," he whimpered.

The Guru turned to look at him squarely and stood to his full height. He was a tall man, especially for India, tall and all lean muscle. Years of yoga had slowly and methodically formed him into a perfect male yogic specimen of health.

He looked at Bob with dark, unfathomable eyes and repeated, "I said you may go."

Bob knew not to contradict him.

Anyway, what would be the point? he asked himself. *I came here out of love, but love I have not received in return.*

He closed the door sadly and walked to the end of the guru's beautiful, tender garden. Tears of sorrow and disappointment streamed down his already wet face.

How could he be so cruel when I give him everything I am?

The words choked in his throat. Then he got angry. Throwing his sacred books on the ground, he jumped on them for good measure and stormed off for the arduous trip home, vowing never to return.

Unknown to Bob, the Master watched him through the window. A tear also ran down the guru's face.

He turned to one of his disciples and said, "He came so close. So very close. If only he would let me crack him."

CHAPTER 13
AJNA TEMPLE

In Prana Community:

Perched on the cliff, Ajna Temple was the masterpiece of Prana Community. The dome-shaped temple was built by Bob Owens and community members several decades ago. Bob always said that the special energy of the temple came from a carefully-orchestrated consecration by his guru.

The consecration was focused on the large, round, black-granite linga, which was front and centre of the temple. *Linga* is the Sanskrit word for a sacred symbol of Divinity. It is believed that lingas develop their own specific power to heal and transform.

As we already know, Bob's relationship with his guru was not always smooth sailing. However, once you have met your guru, you are done for. Once you have fallen in love with a guru, there's no going back. Oh, you can, for sure, leave. You can even say that you hate them. Worse, you can say you were mistaken and that they aren't your guru at all. But you can never *really* leave. The magnetic love of a true guru will always be with you because gurus never stop loving their chosen ones. If you come to them and they say yes, the guru knows that whatever stupid thing you may (and probably will) do, they will not stop loving you. Never. Ever. They cannot escape from you, so it is only fair that you cannot escape from them.

Silence was maintained inside Ajna Temple. The custom was to wash your feet at the entrance, walk slowly through the narrow passage with specially constructed cement flooring containing many acupuncture pressure-point triggers, and sit quietly in front of the linga. Lingas are meant for meditation. You don't pray to a linga. You merge with a linga. You let the linga enter you.

Every fifteen minutes, a chime sounded, and you could choose to leave or remain for another session. You couldn't leave mid-session. Whatever uncomfortable thing you were dealing with, you had to keep dealing with it until the fifteen minutes were up.

The temple design was modelled on the energy system running through all human bodies. The prana or life force of the individual runs along the spine from the base to the crown of the head.

The chakras are centralised locations of swirling, subtle energy channels which play a vital role in the health and functioning of the person. One of these energy centres is not superior to another. They all must function optimally for the well-being of the whole individual.

1. **Muladhara** is the earth element at the base of the spine. It governs the primal urges of food, sleep, sex, and self-preservation and gives a sense of groundedness and stability.
2. **Svadhisthana** is at the pelvis and is the water element. It is associated with creativity, emotions, sexual energy, and the unconscious.
3. **Manipura** is the fire element at the navel. It is the centre of personal power and helps us live with courage and determination.
4. **Anahata** is the air element at the heart. It is the centre of emotion and unconditional love.
5. **Vishuddha** is the ether or space element at the base of the throat. Its function is to help us find authentic self-expression.
6. **Ajna** is between the eyebrows and is not associated with an element, as it is beyond the physical domain. It is the centre of intuition, self-assurance, and inner knowing.
7. **Sahasrara** is above the crown and is also not aligned with a physical element. It is pure consciousness and Divine energy.

Ajna Temple was obviously named after the Ajna chakra. Like the chakra, the temple was a place for deep inner development and spiritual connection.

Although the temple was dedicated to one of the higher, more ethereal chakras, one particular group that frequented the temple was wholeheartedly dedicated to the lower chakras. They were the Manipura Dancers. They were wild. It was the only time that noise was allowed in the temple. They were a damn noisy lot. Noisy and wild.

Everyone loved them.

CHAPTER 14
MANIPURA DANCERS

At Ajna Temple:

Merlyn could hear chimes, bells, and gongs as she approached Ajna Temple by the narrow path along the cliff face. It was the much-anticipated monthly gathering of the Manipura Dancers.

A small group of community members sat under a tree with their Tibetan instruments. They weren't really musicians. Anyone could play the instruments, and there wasn't a music score. You could probably say they were as much musicians as the summer evening breeze racing noisily up and down the cliff, the screeching gliders swooshing from limb to limb, and the chorus of ringing crickets that had replaced the incessant daytime cicada racket (leaving far too small a space of quiet).

Seeing Esther enter the temple, Merlyn followed in pursuit through the foot-washing station, over the acupuncture hallway, and onto one of the mats strategically placed around the circular temple. The professional musicians inside were beating out a strong, rhythmic pulse.

Merlyn was a little surprised by how loud it was and how earthy, physical, and even sexual it was in a temple of such high spiritual vibration. She wondered if the linga objected. Nothing was explained. The music throbbed, hypnotised, and seduced. What it was seducing and for what purpose, Merlyn wasn't sure.

The Manipura Dancers were like Sufi dancers—wild and ecstatic. However, unlike Sufi dancers, they didn't just twirl in endless circles. They moved everywhere and with everything, especially with their hips, core, and the lower part of their bodies.

Ah, thought Merlyn, *that's why they are called the Manipura Dancers. It's the powerhouse fire element coming from the centre.*

Before long, people began joining in the dance. Merlyn glanced around. Throwing caution to the wind, she bounced up from her mat and merged with the throbbing mass. It wasn't so much an exercise in community bonding, although it looked like a party. Essentially, everyone danced within themselves. With love but independently. With abandon but self-contained. Completely free but not crazy. Round and round the linga. More recklessly. More internally. More externally. Swirling, stamping, and mesmerising.

The music, the temple, the linga, and all the bodies seemed to be committed to a process that was intrinsically familiar and also utterly mysterious.

After two hours, thoroughly exhausted and happy, everyone left the temple. Again, Merlyn saw Esther in the distance. She was fairly sure that Esther had seen her too, but she didn't seem to want to talk to her.

Why? Merlyn wondered. *I'm not her client anymore. Only Ben is. So, why doesn't she want to talk to me?*

THE RIGHT HOUSE

CHAPTER 15
INVASION

I*n Waldmeer:*
Summer was in the thick of things, smack-bang in the middle of Waldmeer. The tourists had taken over the little town, as they always did at this time of year.

The locals oscillated between threatening to run them over and reminding themselves that the businesses would not survive without the summer trade. They cursed the noise, rubbish, traffic jams, and "obnoxious, selfish, self-entitled" city-dwellers. The long-term business owners pleaded with their fellow locals to be patient and polite. They coaxed them along with, *A smile costs nothing.* They reminded them that most visitors would only be around for six weeks, and then they would have their beloved town to themselves again.

One group of critters who adored this time of year was the cockatoos. They virtually had a six-week food coma from the overflowing piles of rubbish—yet another point of contention. The Council. *Why don't they collect the rubbish more often? What are we paying rates for?* Oh, yes, it was a six-week grumble-fest. Luckily, the tourists were blissfully (self-ishly) unaware of it.

It wasn't pleasant being in Waldmeer at this time of year. Also, Merlyn's adopted dogs were becoming more restless and problematic in the tiny, rented unit. So she decided to take up a residential offer from Prana Community. If she worked for the community and its outreach programs, she could live and eat there for free. No one in the community was paid, but everyone was supported. They were, however, expected to devote themselves fully to *the work* for the good of all. It was communism at its purest. Merlyn liked things simple and pure. Once again, this time with Bertie and Bella, she moved.

There was one more reason for Merlyn's decision to move. Although summer and the tourist invaders were well and truly in Waldmeer, Ben was not. He said it was the dogs. And the tiny flat. And the combination of the two. It wasn't.

CHAPTER 16
SINGLE FEMALES

Esther stared at Ben. She knew it wasn't appropriate or professional, but she didn't care. She reached over and placed her hand on his thigh. Ben didn't pull away. He stared back at her. Esther's dark eyes and long, black curls framed her perfect face perfectly. At that moment, she seemed to Ben about the most perfect a woman could get—beautiful, intelligent, professionally accomplished, and emotionally open to him. It wasn't clear who moved first, but they somehow ended up together, lips upon the other. One little moment. One momentous moment.

In Prana Community:
　　　Merlyn woke with a start from her dream. She had trouble orienting herself. A rooster crowed grandly with the confidence that only the ignorant and innocent can

have. She remembered that she was in one of the houses of Prana Community. It was an all-female house.

The houses were divided into family groupings, single males, and single females. The whole thing seemed rather antiquated, as if it belonged to a fundamentalist Christian community, not an ashram. However, the community ran by the guru's rules, not by Bob Owens's, but by the real guru—the guru of the guru.

Hearing Bertie and Bella's early morning panting and shuffling, Merlyn prepared to get up and let them outside.

It was just a dream, she reassured herself.

The more she told herself that that was what it was, the less she believed it. The trouble was that the dream made perfect sense—Ben's lack of interest in coming to see her, Esther's interest in avoiding her, Ben's uncharacteristic continued attendance at his psychology sessions, and, as much as Merlyn didn't like seeing it, the natural (almost inevitable) pull between two people like Ben and Esther.

As Merlyn waited for the dogs to finish sniffing around the dew-wet grass, she watched the waning moon on the western horizon. The sun would soon be up on the other side of the sky—no room for both.

Last night's dream wasn't Merlyn's first lucid dream since moving to Prana Community. Many new extrasensory abilities seemed to have awoken in her. It would have frightened her, except that she was living in such a spiritually supportive environment where the supernatural dimension was openly discussed and cultivated.

She weighed up the likelihood of her dream being a meaningless jumble of unconscious thoughts, simply finding a mental outlet. Just as she didn't know whether her dream was true or not, she also did not know, if true, whether it was prophetic of a future event or referring to a past one. Regardless, what could not be ignored was that the dream had confronted Merlyn with the conscious acknowledgement of a palpable pull between Ben and Esther.

Merlyn knew she couldn't really be angry, although other people would probably rant about ethics and responsibilities (technically, Ben was her husband).

But what is the point of technical love? she thought. *If someone loves us, don't we want them to love us, untechnically, with their heart, commitment, breath, and perseverance?*

"Come on, Bertie. Here, Bella," she said as she stood at the back door of the single-female community house. "I guess we are in the right house, after all."

SHAMBHAVI

.

CHAPTER 17
LOOK AT ME

Twice a day, Prana Community members were expected to do a forty-five-minute program of:

1. asanas, which are physical exercises
2. kriyas, which are breathing practices
3. bandhas, which are energy locks
4. and meditation

Much of it was in lotus position (cross-legged on the floor) or some version thereof. That, in itself, was hard, unless you were Eastern. For most Westerners, there were many problems with lotus position—hips that weren't open enough, legs that went numb (and you weren't meant to move), and cores that weren't strong enough to maintain a straight spine.

The sitting posture was only the first problem. Then there were the asanas or physical postures. They were demanding. The kriyas or breathing exercises were even more challenging. Merlyn usually felt that she was about to drown from lack of oxygen, which sent her into panic mode and made her breathing even shallower. Locking the bandhas or energy points in the body seemed like it was meant for yogis who lived in caves. Merlyn had no idea if the invisible bandhas she was trying to target were hit or missed. The thought crossed her mind more than once, *Are they even real?*

There was the option of joining the guided classes run by Veronica, Verloren's daughter. Veronica's yoga skills were out of this world, and her perfectly sculptured body was a testament to the long-term benefits of the practice. She was a very attractive woman around Merlyn's age. Merlyn didn't warm to her. She wanted to, but it didn't happen. After a while, Merlyn realised that it probably didn't happen with most people.

In some ways, Veronica and her mother were alike. Both had lots of life force, were intelligent (not overly so, but more intelligent than the average person), and were highly driven. In other ways, they were different. Verloren was a warm person. Merlyn wouldn't call her a *loving* person because love is inclusive of everyone and has no ulterior motive. Warmth is an emotional attitude towards chosen people. Nevertheless, it is a good quality, and while Verloren had it, her daughter did not. Veronica wasn't mean (her mother still could be), but she was empty. She had never invested in her emotional connection. Perhaps, she did not know how to.

Neither mother nor daughter ever looked Merlyn directly in the eyes. Whether or not someone was capable of and willing to look at Merlyn was her quickest measure of them. It was unfailingly accurate.

CHAPTER 18
DANCING IS MY RELIGION

I*n Ajna Temple:*
One morning, Merlyn decided to do her yoga practice in Ajna Temple. So long as you were quiet, it was permitted. The temple was empty. She started enthusiastically, but soon deteriorated. In the middle of the kriyas, she gasped for air. Hearing a muffled laugh behind her, she turned to see Shambhavi. He was Veronica's husband. Looking around to ensure no one else was in the no-speak temple, he whispered hello and moved towards Merlyn.

"It's hard at first," said Shambhavi sympathetically. "When Veronica and I started dating, she brought me here to the community. Even though I come from a dancing family, I struggled. Then, one day, here in the temple, I had an idea. I started to turn all my dancing knowledge into yoga. I didn't tell anyone, but I came in here every day and worked on my experiment. When I was ready, I told Veronica, and that was the day that the Manipura Dancers were born. That was also how I got my name, which means *some-*

thing that is born from happiness. They said that when I dance, something blissful comes alive in me."

After a pause, he said, "Dancing is my religion," and recited this poem.

Dancing is my yoga.
I do it every day.
Ancient as the Eastern one;
highway and gateway.

Proper posture.
Straight spine.
Lit up, heated up.
Fire is mine.

Free-flow energy.
Life-force flow.
Open the channels,
activate the glow.

When I'm walking,
I'm rumba-ing along.
Running for the bus,
cha-cha-ing like a song.

Pay attention
or left will trip up right.
Pay attention
or partner will fight.

Spine up.
Step up.

Close up.
Burn up.

She watched as much as listened because he was dancing as much as speaking. Her mind turned to Veronica, *Like her or not, we are all here together.*

Merlyn remembered a section in the community book of the guru's teachings.

ALL THE POSITIONS YOU LEARN IN YOGA ARE DONE IN ORDER TO LEARN HOW TO NOT TAKE POSITIONS IN LIFE. YOU LIKE THIS PERSON. YOU DON'T LIKE THAT ONE. LIFE MUST BE SEEN FRESHLY. EVERYTHING IS A POSSIBILITY. WHEN I SEE YOU, I LOOK AT YOU FRESHLY. WHAT ARE YOU AT THIS MOMENT? WE MUST GET RID OF ALL OUR POSITIONS. THAT IS A GREAT WEIGHT GONE.

PART III
BORDERFIRMA

NO GOING BACK

CHAPTER 19
TRAVELLING TRIO

Eight months ago, after a twenty-year absence from Borderfirma, Rybert decided to finish what he had started and ventured back through the Cypress Lane portal. Unknown to him, he had reopened the inactive Floating Cave bell portal. However, no sooner was he back in Borderfirma than he had to return to Waldmeer with Faith, who had not been able to get back to Earth in all that time.

After several months with Malik's family in Waldmeer, Faith decided to return to the Borderfirma Mountains to see why Gabriel hadn't come to Earth. She had assumed it would be the first thing he would do once Odin informed him that the bell portal was open.

As his recent trip to Borderfirma had only been two days, Rybert decided to go, too. He asked Tom to manage the Wurt Wurt Koort Tearooms and said he wanted to travel. Faith's thirteen-year-old granddaughter, Maria, was an unexpected but welcome addition to the travelling trio.

Six months ago, in the inter-dimensional Borderfirma Lowlands: In the middle of winter, the three intrepid travellers (Faith, Rybert, and Maria) stood below the ancient portal bell of Floating Cave Monastery with the equally ancient monk looking on.

"Welcome back, Lady Faith and Rybert," said the monk with eyes resembling Floating Cave's mystical waters. "I've been waiting for you."

He walked towards Maria and peered at her. *Into* her would be more accurate.

He nodded approvingly and said with a half-smile and a half-bow, "Welcome, Lady Maria. Your father, young Malik, has done a good job."

Faith laughed and said, "*Young* Malik is now in his mid-forties."

"That's still young in my books," laughed the monk.

Rybert thought it was probably true, given that the monk appeared over one hundred years old.

As the trio and the monk walked happily towards the peeling, green door of the monastery, an almighty crack of lightning smashed the bell behind them and sent them all flying. Unharmed but shocked, they stared at the bell, which lay in a million pieces, so small that the wind was already taking them away in a swirling funnel. They stood in amazement until the last of the pieces had lifted into the ether to return to some place that was, no doubt, fitting and proper, although none of them knew where. Not even the monk.

"Well, I'll be," chuckled the monk. "I thought I was beyond being surprised."

Faith's thoughts had already turned to the immediate consequences of the portal's destruction. She could not get Maria back to her parents as she had promised. Rybert also would not be able to return to Earth. She was sure he would have intended this trip to be an adventure, not an inter-dimensional lifestyle change. She thought about Gabriel and his whereabouts. She had not seen Gabriel in Wald-meer, but that didn't necessarily mean he had not gone to Earth. She turned worried eyes to the monk.

"Gabriel is in the Borderfirma Mountains," said the monk calmly.

Not knowing what else to do, all four went to the monastery kitchen, down the hallway, second door on the left. Rybert glanced a few doors down to the room he slept in on his first visit to the Borderfirma Lowlands. One night was by himself, and the next was with his most unwilling and begrudging roommate, Gabriel. He couldn't help smiling at the memory.

"We will think about it all tomorrow," said the monk as he busied himself with making tea and toast.

In that environment of the monastery, where everything always seemed in its right place, the travelling trio decided to do just that—think about it tomorrow.

CHAPTER 20
THIRTEEN

The next morning, the Lowlands was abuzz with news of the travelling trio. Aristotle sent word to the monastery with greetings and requests.

Hello Mum, Rybert, and Maria,

Indra and I are so pleased and relieved that you are back safely, Mum. What a treat that we finally get to meet our niece, Maria. Can't wait! And, of course, Rybert, I remember how good you were to my family when we were all in Waldmeer twenty years ago. We missed seeing you on your last stint in the Lowlands because you were no sooner here than Mum took you back to Waldmeer with her. We are sorry to hear that the portal has been destroyed, but we have some suggestions.

Firstly, give us Maria! Gabriel looked after me on Earth when I was around the same age as Maria.

He probably doesn't want another thirteen-year-old
to look after. As you know, Indra and I have made
the conscious decision not to have children because
we consider that our duties are already very high
with caring for the Lowlands people. Maria, however,
would be an exception as she is exceptional. The
Borderfirma Mountains already has plenty of spiritual leverage, but here in the Lowlands, even after
thirteen years as rulers, we still struggle to keep the
people on the right track. Maria would be a valuable
help, particularly as she matures.

Secondly, give us Rybert! We know he didn't
intend to stay, but that is how it is. Rybert is
wonderful with people, all sorts of people. He under-
stands them and connects with them. Indra and I
would like to invite him to take up the esteemed position of People's Advisor. He will be one of our most
trusted and important inner-circle people.

Expectantly,
Aristotle
Ruler of the Borderfirma Lowlands

NOTE:

After Gabriel and thirteen-year-old Aristotle travelled to
Earth many years ago via the picture frame portal, Aristotle's
father, Zufar, took Indra away. He kept her away for ten
Borderfirma years, equalling the few months Aristotle was
on Earth. It was essential for the future of the Lowlands for

Aristotle and Indra to remain the same age. After all, the stars were so aligned for their togetherness that they were born on the same day. When Aristotle returned to Borderfirma, Zufar brought Indra back, and they were inseparable ever since.

CHAPTER 21
ONE MORE DAY

"I might be good with people," Rybert complained to Faith the following morning, "but that doesn't mean I like them."

The new travelling trio of Rybert, Maria, and Odin were leaving the monastery for the Lowlands palace.

"It will be good for you," said Faith encouragingly. "And you can keep an eye on Maria."

"We won't be needing help with Maria," said Odin. "I think I've always been a competent guardian of the royal children."

"Of course, you have been," said Faith, "but, you know, we are all getting older, and I'm sure you would be glad of a little help."

"Rybert isn't exactly a spring chicken, himself," Odin muttered as he gathered the last of the things.

"Be careful," said Faith to Rybert as she kissed him good-bye. "I'll visit you soon."

LATER THAT DAY, Faith passed the Borderfirma Lowlands exit sign of two snakes. During Evanora's rule, the intertwined snakes were attacking each other with poison and strangulation. After the Borderfirma Battle, the sign changed to an image of two snakes in a peaceful figure-eight pattern. When Faith passed the Borderfirma Mountains entry sign, she read,

If you must dream a dream,
at least make it a happy one.

Word had been sent that Gabriel would meet Faith at Odin's cottage in the Great Valley. The cottage was halfway between Floating Cave Monastery and the Borderfirma Mountains palace. It would take Gabriel and Faith a day to walk from their respective positions to the cottage.

It was strange that some things about Borderfirma were so advanced and others were almost primitive. The mental, emotional, psychic, and spiritual state of most Borderfirmarians was significantly evolved (not so much in the Lowlands). However, little investment was made in machinery, technology, and many other aspects of modern living. For instance, there were no cars. Most everyone walked everywhere. The Wise Ones said this unique balance gave Borderfirma its special purpose in the universe.

As Faith drew closer to Odin's cottage in the Great Valley, she remembered things that Nina (Odin's mother) often said about her beloved forest, such as:

"People who don't live in the forest often have a romantic ideal of it, but if you sit under a tree, every insect within a ten-metre radius will make a beeline for you. It's not romantic. It is, however, transformative. To feel its pulse, its rhythm, its life. To learn its ways, its regenerative power, and its creative prowess.

When we look at trees, we think of them as trunks, branches, and leaves. We forget that under the ground is a vast and complex system of intertwined roots that is as large and fascinating as the system above the soil. It is through this underground system that the trees talk to each other, warn each other of danger, help the sick trees, support the elderly ones, and generally have an elaborate and purposeful way of communicating with the whole ecological community."

Faith's thoughts were interrupted by Gabriel, who had seen her in the distance and come to meet her. After an all-day walk in the forest, they were both deeply peaceful.

"The cottage isn't as clean and tidy as when Nina was here," said Gabriel, "but it'll be fine for the night."

Once inside, Faith felt there was still a strong sense of Nina's warm and wise presence in the house. Actually, Faith had felt Nina walking beside her for the last few hours.

"Amira, do you think you'll be able to walk the whole way back to the palace tomorrow?" Gabriel asked.

After all these years, Gabriel still called Faith by the name he knew her by on Earth—Amira. Indeed, he first knew her as Maria, and it took him a long time to adjust to her acquired name of Amira. Faith felt it was enough to ask of him. Anyway, being called Amira reminded her of another side of herself to the role she had in Borderfirma as Lady Faith.

"I think I'll be fine," she said.

"If not," said Gabriel, "we can stay here one more day."

GOING BACK

CHAPTER 22
OLD FRIEND

B*ack to now, in Waldmeer:*
One end-of-summer morning, after Farkas's dance aerobics class at the Waldmeer Warriors, Merlyn decided to stay and chat with her older friend, Ide.

Merlyn had become so immersed in her life at Prana Community that she hadn't been outside its perimeter since moving there. She wasn't sure if her self-imposed isolation was due to an increased desire for spiritual progress or if it was a way of avoiding the pain of Ben's relationship with Esther. Either way, it now seemed sensible to re-enter the world, even though that meant an hour-and-a-half drive for a single dance class.

She had hardly danced for the past year. Her intensive adult ballet training stopped when she moved to Store Creek, and she had only been to a few of the Waldmeer Warrior dance classes before moving to Prana Community. She did participate in the rollicking fun of the Manipura Dancers of Ajna Temple, but that was only once a month.

Pulling the body back into dance mode takes considerable effort.

Even though Merlyn and Ide had only met a few times, they were like old friends.

"How are you, darling?" asked Ide. "Are you enjoying life in the commune?"

"Definitely," said Merlyn.

"I envy you a little," smiled Ide. "It took Bob Owens ten years to build Ajna Temple, right at the beginning of the community's life. Even though I never lived in the ashram, I knew Bob and sometimes visited his property to see how it was all going. I was always that way inclined, although the rest of Waldmeer thought he had gone raving mad. I remember when Farkas and I got together, he was not a fan of Bob. Nor was he a fan of Salt. He got over that. By now, I think he has got over a lot of things."

Merlyn remembered that it would be a year since Salt passed on.

"Did Salt like Ajna Temple?" asked Merlyn.

"He loved it," said Ide. "It was right up his alley."

Merlyn looked closely at Ide, who showed no sign of residual grief.

"You remember the good times you had with Salt rather than missing him, don't you?" ventured Merlyn.

"Every moment is a gift, sweetheart. But when the moment passes, the gift is not gone. The real gift, you see, is the life and spirit within another. That life is everywhere around us. It gets concentrated in a certain place, and we call that a *loved one*. But if the *loved one* has to journey some-where, we haven't lost the gift of love or life. It swirls around and shows itself to us in a million ways. Look at the sea shining. Isn't it brilliant? Isn't it perfect? How could we not be happy to see it and live alongside it?"

Farkas appeared at the gym door and said, "I'll be one more minute, Ide. I forgot to do something."

Merlyn wondered if Ide and Farkas were back together. It seemed too personal a question to ask of a senior couple.

Ide pointed towards the door where Farkas had just stood and said, "I enjoy what the ocean brings, but I don't insist on anything. Nature has seasons. After all this time, Farkas and I have been able to enjoy each other without any stress. Recently, I even asked him if he would like to share the same house, mine or his. I'm no longer attached to houses."

Merlyn was very interested to know what his response was.

"He said that he has to go somewhere soon," said Ide with a slight frown, "and that an old friend has been calling in."

"Who?" asked Merlyn.

"A woman called Milyaket," said Ide. "I could see that Farkas was quite enamoured with her, so I asked him if she was a love interest?"

"And?" asked Merlyn.

"He laughed," said Ide, "and said that Milyaket is not that sort of a woman."

CHAPTER 23
GREAT VALLEY

I
n the inter-dimensional *Borderfirma Mountains:*
Gabriel's "one more day" in the Great Valley turned into one more, one more, and one more. Gabriel and Amira had been living there since winter, and it was now the end of summer.

At first, Amira said her legs were tired and that she couldn't walk back to the Borderfirma Mountains palace straight away. While she recovered, they settled into life in the forest. Amira busied herself with cleaning and sorting Odin's cottage, while Gabriel had an endless array of jobs in the large garden around the house. It was a never-ending task to keep the forest from reclaiming the house. Odin had hardly been in the cottage since Nina's passing, so the forest reclaiming was well underway.

This precious time in the Great Valley was the most uninterrupted time Amira and Gabriel had ever spent together over the three decades of knowing each other, being together, and not being together.

"Why didn't you go to Earth when Rybert opened the

bell portal?" asked Amira one morning. "I thought it would be the first thing you would do after all these years of complaining about being stuck here."

"Because bloody Odin took forever to tell me what happened," said Gabriel.

"But eventually, he told you," said Amira, "and you still didn't come."

"I wanted to," said Gabriel. "Every day, for weeks, I told myself that I would return to Earth the following day, but the following day came, and I didn't go. I was a bit afraid."

"Of what?" asked Amira. "You have had to face many fears, but I would have thought that the prospect of returning home would not have been one of them."

"I was afraid that if I went," said Gabriel, "I wouldn't come back. It was such a mammoth decision to come here. It took all the courage I had. I was losing everything familiar, everything I knew—except you."

He turned towards the forest and listened, an ability he had only acquired in recent years.

"However, it wasn't just that," continued Gabriel. "I realised that many people come to me with their problems here in Borderfirma [Gabriel was often sought for his warmth, support, and advice]. I know I can't help them like you because, well... you are you, but I can help in a different way. I may not be the most mature person in the world, but I hope I have learned something."

CHAPTER 24
PUTTING THE
WORLD TO SLEEP

I n *Waldmeer:*
It was nice to see Merlyn in class today, thought Farkas as he lay in bed. *It was a good day.*

Nothing happened of any significance, but he felt good all day. Looking out the window, he could see a blanket of stars gently putting this part of the world to sleep.

"Are you ready?" asked Milyaket of the inter-dimensional Homeland as the starlight illuminated her translucent, ageless body.

"As ready as I can be," said Farkas nervously.

"And you understand," said Milyaket, "that it is a one-way journey this time?"

Farkas nodded.

"Do you remember what I told you when you first came here to Waldmeer?" asked Milyaket.

"Yes," said Farkas. "That I would make better progress with a human body."

"And something else," said Milyaket.

"You said that we see the separation of life as very arbitrary," said Farkas, "and that we have far more connection than we are even vaguely aware of."

"And that you will not lose the love that is yours," said Milyaket.

"What is that love?" asked Farkas. "Is it someone?"

"Partly," said Milyaket, "but mostly not."

Farkas walked to the window and said, "It's what the stars do."

Milyaket gestured that it was time to go. Farkas allowed himself to be pulled away with her. Blind trust, if it is trust in the right thing, can make some things painless.

CHAPTER 25
HOMEWARD BOUND

I n the *Borderfirma Mountains:*
"You know how I've been telling you that Nina often talks to me?" said Amira that evening in bed.

"You've been telling me," said Gabriel, "but I never see her."

"Today, she told me that the frame may work again," said Amira.

"What frame?" asked Gabriel. "Work for what?"

"Zufar's frame," said Amira. "The one that took you and Aristotle to Earth."

"You mean," said Gabriel, "that it may work as a portal?"

"Perhaps," said Amira.

"I don't know why you are telling me that now," said Gabriel.

"I'm just letting you know what she said," said Amira. "In case you ever wanted a change of scene."

"I'm too old for a change of scene," joked Gabriel.

"Sixty isn't old," said Amira. "People have started their

most important life work at that age. Also, remember that the travelling trio are coming tomorrow."

As Amira and Gabriel hadn't been outside the Great Valley since arriving, their loved ones from the Borderfirma Mountains and Lowlands occasionally visited.

"One more thing," said Amira.

"Hmm?" said Gabriel sleepily.

"I love you very much," said Amira.

She didn't often say those words. She lived them, but she didn't tend to say them. She held Gabriel's hand and watched him drift away.

THE NEXT MORNING:

Gabriel woke to birdcall and was surprised to feel Amira's hand still on his.

That's strange, he thought. *Amira's hand is cold. The bed is warm.*

He sat bolt upright and stared at her. She was dead.

SEVERAL HOURS LATER:

Gabriel had been sitting, almost motionless, for several hours. His mind was anything but motionless. At first, he thought that if he just sat there and waited, Amira would somehow return. To his horror, every passing hour cemented how truly dead her body was. He got up and paced the room. There was no point in finding someone to tell. It would take too long. And what could they do? Besides, he knew that the travelling trio would be at the cottage by late afternoon.

How, on Earth, am I going to tell them that Amira is dead? he thought.

"How on Earth," he repeated out loud.

He went to Nina's old bedroom and frantically rummaged through her countless possessions from every nook and cranny of the Universe. Behind the wardrobe—the frame! Placing it next to his and Amira's bed, he wondered if it would work.

If it does work, he thought, *is it cowardice to go? To leave Amira here for the trio to find? To leave the people of the Borderfirma Mountains when they have lost her?*

He felt the pull of the frame. Was it cowardice? He didn't know. All he knew was that if he went to Earth, the intense pain he was feeling right now had a better chance of dissipating. He also knew from experience that, with time, his memories of Borderfirma and Amira would dull.

Early evening, at Odin's cottage:
Maria had been crying for the past hour.

"I want to go back to Mummy and Daddy," she kept sobbing.

Rybert tried to pacify her, but he was crying, too. Odin wasn't crying. He was too distraught.

"The frame must be working again," said Odin as his gaze alternated between his lifelong-beloved deceased queen and the frame.

Maria moved towards the frame, obviously intending to use it as a portal. Rybert grabbed her hand.

"You can't go, my love," he said. "We don't know, for sure, where it goes."

Maria may have been full of sweetness and light, but she was her grandmother's granddaughter, and she got that look in her eye. She leapt for the frame. Rybert wouldn't let go. Anyway, he knew he didn't want to be in Borderfirma without Faith, and Tom would surely be sick of managing the Wurt Wurt Koort Tearooms by now. Odin felt that there was no way he could live in the Borderfirma Mountains without his mother, Lady Faith, and a royal child to protect. Maria had brought the spark of life back into his existence. They were always together. He grabbed Rybert's hand, and the travelling trio were off. Odin on Earth? God help them both!

IN THE HOMELAND:

Amira moved along the light path to the Homeland. Although Nina had been speaking to her for months, she had only recently told her that it was time to return to the Homeland. In the distance, Farkas and Milyaket were moving in the same direction as Amira. She saw them, and they saw her, "saw" in the way that souls see.

PART IV
MANDALA

MAHASHIVRATRI

CHAPTER 26
DANCING THE DARK AWAY

*A*t the Waldmeer Warriors, in Waldmeer:

After Farkas's recent passing, Ide remembered the Manipura Dancers. She had not been to Prana Community for years, but contacted them through Merlyn, and Shambhavi was sent as the new Waldmeer Warrior's dance teacher. His first class went as well as could be expected.

"Thank you for a wonderful class," said Shambhavi. "It's been a pleasure working with you."

He knew these initial classes would be make or break for such a small, insular town as Waldmeer. He brought out all his charm to try and gently win them over. Although he was way overqualified for such a class, he wanted to use the opportunity to build a bridge between Waldmeer and Prana Community. The former had always been deeply suspicious of the latter. Besides, Shambhavi not only loved to dance, but he also loved to teach.

"If anyone would like to join us for Mahashivratri tonight," said Shambhavi, "you would be very welcome."

Prana Community was nondenominational but celebrated many of the Hindu traditions of Bob Owens's Indian guru, including numerous moon-related ones. In the same way the moon affects the tides, its gravitational pull affects other water forms, including the water in us.

Shivratri is the darkest night of the lunar month as it immediately precedes the new moon. Mahashivratri is the most important Shivratri of the year. There is a natural upsurge of energy due to the position of the planets. It is honoured as the night when Shiva danced the darkness away. The idea is to stay awake all night in an upright position with a straight spine. Mahashivratri was generally a mixture of meditation, talks, and exuberant celebration to aid the night-long wakefulness.

The normal monthly performances of the Manipura Dancers were always scheduled for either the new moon (Shivratri) or full moon (Purnima). It depended on what they felt their focus needed to be.

They used the full moon nights to concentrate on physical and mental activation, positivity, life force, the beginning of various projects, and to improve health and vitality. They joked that the full moon brought out the madness in them all. Although it was a joke, there was some truth in it. Creation of any sort needs a little bit of madness.

They used the new-moon nights when they needed more introspection, healing, inner work, and alignment.

"Mahashivratri is the darkest night," said Shambhavi, "but we don't focus on the dark. We look towards the coming light. We'll have a midnight meditation at Ajna Temple, and the rest of the night, we'll be singing and dancing."

He added with a sparkling smile, "It's a party! Just like Shiva, we dance the dark away."

CHAPTER 27
FULL HOUSE

After the dance class, Ide told Merlyn, "It's exciting to be visiting Prana Community tonight for Mahashivratri. I'll try to talk Gabriel into coming with me."

"Who is Gabriel?" asked Merlyn.

"He's my friend from many years ago," said Ide.

When they were around forty, Ide and Amira were close friends. Their little circle included Amira's partner at that time, Gabriel, and Ide's partner at that time, Farkas.

"When I was with Farkas," said Ide, "we were friends with Amira and her on-again/off-again partner, Gabriel."

"I say *we*," smiled Ide, "but Farkas didn't really befriend anyone much. A few chosen ones—that was it. He had a sort of love-hate relationship with Amira, and I don't think he cared much for Gabriel."

Word soon spread in Waldmeer that the reclusive but respected man on the hill, Farkas, had unexpectedly died. Further, Gabriel, the artist who had lived and worked in the area and then mysteriously disappeared more than twenty years ago, was back. Apparently, his return to Waldmeer was prompted by the death of Amira (originally Maria, daughter of local fisherman Lenny). She hadn't been seen for even longer than Gabriel.

Malik's house was more than full when not only Gabriel turned up to relay the sad news of Malik's mother's passing, but before the day was done, the travelling trio of Maria, Rybert, and Odin also arrived. Malik's sorrow at losing his mother, Faith-Amira, was softened by his joy at the safe return of his daughter, Maria. Reconnecting with Odin, Malik's childhood guru from the Great Valley, was an added emotional surprise. The house was indeed full and full of personalities.

Rybert stayed one night and was then very happy to return to Wurt Wurt Koort, whereupon Tom was very happy to return to his life in the city.

Ide offered Gabriel a room in her house, saying, "You need a home until you re-establish yourself, and I need company."

Ide's house was much quieter than Malik's, and Gabriel was drawn to its creative energy. Also, as Ide was an old friend of Amira's, he felt it was a safe place to recover from Amira's passing and restart his life on Earth.

He had already decided to take up his former passion for art. Although Ide was happy to have Gabriel's company, she wasn't Amira. She didn't love Gabriel like Amira. The friendship between Ide and Gabriel was one that both would have to work at if they were to be compatible housemates.

When Ide asked Gabriel about going to Mahashivratri, he said he had already had *the darkest night of the year*. However, having little to lose and wanting to invest in a new start, he decided to go anyway.

CHAPTER 28
RITUALS AND DRAMA

In Prana Community:

Shambhavi hadn't told his Waldmeer Warrior dance students about the extensive personal preparations that Prana Community members (including Merlyn) were undergoing for Mahashivratri. There had been several weeks of intermittent fasting, chanting, meditation, and preparing the body, mind, and heart for the blessings of the night.

The most significant preparation was the Pancha Bhuta Kriya. It was essentially a process of integrating the body with the fundamental aspects of Earth existence.

Pancha Bhuta Kriya

1. **Abhaya Sutra**—yellow cotton thread dipped in turmeric paste worn for a mandala period of forty days. It was tied around the wrist and knotted three times. After the mandala period, it was

carefully removed (without cutting) and either tied to a flowering tree or dug into the earth.

2. **Vastram**—black cotton shawl with Tamil writing worn during meditation sessions.

3. **Bhoomi**—prepared grains of soil eaten during one of the meditations.

4. **Vibhuti**—holy ash, which came from the guru's Indian temple, used for rubbing on the chakra points.

5. **The five elements**—earth, water, wind, fire, and space were observed in particular ways. The residents of Prana Community lived hand-in-hand with nature. However, they deliberately deepened their connection during Mahashivratri. They walked barefoot in the sand and on the forest soil. They drank water from copper containers with attentive reverence for its life-sustaining purpose. They swam in the sea, sometimes naked (but this was a contentious point for some). They went for long cliff walks with the wind blasting their troubles away. They stared at the fire of their sacramental candles and open fireplaces. They frequently acknowledged the vast, incomprehensible beauty of the space above and around them.

The Hindu traditions may seem foreign to those of other religious cultures, but most religions are full of rituals, drama, costumes, use of the elements (particularly fire and water), and stories. A full-on Catholic Mass could rival any Hindu celebration with its culture and theatre. Humans are essentially storytellers and dramatists. It helps them connect to their right-brain functions of creativity, emotion, intuition, imagination, expression, and innovative thinking.

Without the Pancha Bhuta Kriya preparations, Mahashivratri would have been a shadow of itself. A lot of its power came from them, but many visitors, with no preparation, attended the festival.

Merlyn saw that Ben and Esther were on the list of expected visitors. She mentally braced for their visit with the prayer that she wished no one harm and could not be adversely affected by other people's decisions or life choices.

Along with the earth, water, wind, fire, and space, it was a mighty prayer.

Was it enough?

Possibly not, but Merlyn knew that without opportunities to grow, we don't.

EQUINOX

CHAPTER 29
MABON

In the northern hemisphere, Mahashivratri immediately precedes the spring equinox (the herald of spring). In Prana Community, Mahashivratri precedes the autumnal equinox (the beginning of autumn). Both equinoxes have the same amount of day as night. Thus, they are a time of transition and reset.

"The autumnal equinox or Mabon is Witches' Thanksgiving," Rybert would say. "It is the end of a year's growth cycle. Everything changes. The trees change colour. They shed their leaves. It's a time of general shedding." He would then add with a wink, "Shedding clothes is also appropriate, but it does depend on who is doing the shedding."

It was around the autumnal equinox, a year ago, that Merlyn moved to Store Creek. She quickly became a frequent visitor to the Wurt Wurt Koort Tearooms. At first, she went to see her friend, Tom, and his Brussels Griffon, Hardy. However, she soon became fond of Rybert as well. Then, she was happy to see either Tom or Rybert. There was a twenty-year age difference between the two gay men, who weren't partners, but it was equally interesting to talk to either. Rybert was older and grumpier, but he was also wiser. Both were engaging and caring, and both were fond of Merlyn.

Before leaving for Borderfirma, Rybert asked Tom and Merlyn to take over his shifts at the cafe. Tom took the bulk of them. Merlyn did some, but that reduced to zero once she moved to Prana Community a few months ago. Although Merlyn wanted to reconnect with Rybert and see how his trip had gone, she also had another reason for visiting him.

In the Wurt Wurt Koort Tearooms:

"You seem different," said Rybert.

"It's living at Prana," said Merlyn. "It would change anyone. You didn't come to Mahashivratri?"

"I have enough of the supernatural in my life," said Rybert, who came from a long line of witches.

"How was it?" he asked.

"Spectacular," said Merlyn. "Heaps of people there. Lots of dancing, chanting, and bare-chested men. Everyone was on their best behaviour and made a big effort to be positive and friendly."

Merlyn fiddled with the yellow thread wound three times around her thin wrist. It had only been there for seven days of the forty-day mandala period.

"Since Mahashivratri," she said, "I have been hearing a voice in the temple." She paused to gauge Rybert's reaction. "The voice only speaks when no one is around and says not to tell anyone."

"Then why are you telling me?" asked Rybert.

"The voice said that she is Amira," said Merlyn.

Not many things surprised Rybert, but he was visibly surprised and moved.

"Faith," he said softly, more to himself than to Merlyn.

"Why do you call her Faith?" asked Merlyn.

"By the time I knew her, she was Faith, Malik's mother," said Rybert. "However, she was Amira for most of her life here."

"What did she say?" asked Rybert.

"That you should come to Ajna Temple," said Merlyn.

CHAPTER 30
HEART PRIORITY

That afternoon, in Ajna Temple:
"She's not saying anything," said Rybert. "Are you sure she is here?"

"She's not saying anything to me either," shrugged Merlyn, "but I think she's here."

After sitting quietly for fifteen minutes and looking at the intensely powerful, black granite linga, Rybert turned his gaze to Merlyn. In this special space with its sacred atmosphere, Merlyn looked beautiful. Rybert thought about Faith. He had always felt that, somehow or other, he had missed out on connecting with Faith in the way he would have liked to. He didn't know if it was him or her or Gabriel or something else. It felt unfinished, incomplete. And now she was gone. The discomfort of it gave him a sudden but clear idea.

"You know what you need?" said Rybert, breaking the mesmeric silence.

"Shhh," said Merlyn. "We're not supposed to talk in here. What? What do I need?"

"A boyfriend," said Rybert.

Merlyn laughed.

"What about me?" said Rybert.

"I don't know if you need a boyfriend," said Merlyn.

"No, silly," said Rybert. "What about me as your boyfriend?"

Merlyn laughed even more.

"You are gay," she said. "Not even bisexual. You are completely gay."

"True," said Rybert, "but I will make an exception."

"Do you even know what to do?" asked Merlyn, smiling.

"Err, how hard can it be?" said Rybert with absolute confidence.

Becoming more serious, he said, "I'm serious. I'm sure I can work it out, but it's not really about that. At sixty, you rule your own body. It doesn't rule you anymore. You tell it what to do, and it does it."

Realising that Rybert was making a genuine offer and was waiting for an answer, Merlyn silently said to Amira, *Now would be a good time to say something.*

"The main thing is the relationship we would have with each other," said Rybert. "No one has to know, unless you want them to. We only have to go as far as we both wish, and either of us can abandon the idea if we find it's not what we want. The important thing is that we would care about each other in a way that is more committed than the average friendship. We would make each other a time priority—a heart priority."

Merlyn heard not a word from Amira but decided to make her own decision and said, "Sold!"

CHAPTER 31
IN THE LAP OF DEVOTION

In the Wurt Wurt Koort Tearooms:

"That's ridiculous," said Tom when Rybert told him about his new girlfriend. "That's the stupidest thing I've ever heard."

"Then," said Rybert, heading for the kitchen with some plates, "you haven't heard many stupid things."

THAT AFTERNOON:

Tom had already returned to the city by the time Merlyn got to the tearooms. She sat in her favourite corner. Although Wurt Wurt Koort was a tiny town, the tearooms were relatively busy. Not only did the locals go there, but the seaside visitors to Waldmeer often stopped at the quaint cafe.

During a quieter moment, Merlyn said to Rybert, "You will never guess who arrived at Prana yesterday."

Rybert shrugged as if that was a silly statement, because it could be anyone.

"Bob Owens's guru!" said Merlyn. "Guru Gadubanud from India."

"I thought he was long since dead," said Rybert.

"We all did," said Merlyn. "He has never before visited Prana Community in person. Apparently, during the building of Ajna Temple, he would occasionally 'appear' in nonphysical form to help Bob with the consecration of the linga. Bob started building that temple when he was sixty, finished it at seventy, died at eighty, and would now be ninety. Everyone assumed the big boss guru would have been older than Bob, but Guru Gadubanud is only seventy. Goes to show that seniority and superiority are not the same thing."

"Why has he come?" asked Rybert.

"He said that the linga needs upkeep, and as we don't know how to care for its energy properly, he decided to come himself. He said he brought his body this time, even though it was more tiring and expensive."

Rybert looked unconvinced and said, "Is that all he is doing? Fixing up the linga?"

"He gave a talk last night in the temple," said Merlyn, "and told us that he would continue to do so every evening until he leaves."

"What did he say?" asked Rybert.

"That he has made himself into a reasonable man," said Merlyn.

"Was he unreasonable before?" asked Rybert.

"Definitely," said Merlyn. "Gurus are like that. They don't care about being reasonable. They can be mental. They only care about one thing—your spiritual progress. They will do whatever seems best to promote that. The guru said that in recent years, as he has limited time left, he has been travelling to the West. He decided to modify his approach so that Westerners would listen to his message."

Rybert moved a pile of cutlery into the kitchen.

As no one else was in the cafe, Merlyn called after him, "He finished the session with a meditation and said, 'I want you to sit in my lap.'"

"That sounds dodgy," said Rybert poking his head around the door.

"No, not like that," said Merlyn. "Gurus aren't like that. Not proper ones. He meant figuratively 'sit', that we must trust him as a young child trusts their parents, if we want to benefit from his presence. No resistance. Absolute devotion to the process. He said that each one must choose the way most suited to their temperament and stage of development, but the quickest way is the way of devotion because whatever we are devoted to, we merge with."

"That sounds unreasonable to me," said Rybert. "What if he takes you somewhere you don't want to go?"

"I know what you mean," said Merlyn, "but the problem is that without the trust, he can't help that much. He said, 'It is your choice how much you will get from my visit. I can guarantee that you will come out of these processes alive and well, but I cannot guarantee that you will all return to your previous lives. It is my wish and blessing that you receive maximum benefit.'"

OMNI-ALL

CHAPTER 32
CLOSER

I n *Prana Community:*
  "How are things going in your community house?"
  asked Shambhavi.

"Fine, thanks," said Merlyn.

She wondered why he was asking, as he had never enquired about her living arrangements before.

"Do you like it?" persisted Shambhavi.

"It's fine," said Merlyn, "for a single female household."

"Veronica and I have an empty bungalow behind our house," said Shambhavi.

Shambhavi and Veronica were one of the few full-time community members who didn't live at Prana. They owned a five-acre property halfway between Prana and Waldmeer. It was as beautiful as Prana and likewise situated on a cliff face overlooking the sea.

"The bungalow has been empty for a while. We think you would be a good person to go into it, considering you have the dogs and all," said Shambhavi. "Also, you seem to be travelling to Waldmeer a lot, and we are closer."

I'm not sure how enthusiastic Veronica would be about this idea, thought Merlyn. *Shambhavi must have talked her into it. He can be convincing when he puts his mind to it. Oh well, that's their affair, not mine. My affair is with life.*

"I'll take it," said Merlyn gratefully. "Thank you."

"It gets you out of the single female house," said Shambhavi.

"It does," said Merlyn. "Actually, I don't consider myself female or single."

"There's not a lot of masculine in you," said Shambhavi.

"Yes, I am a woman who considers herself a woman," said Merlyn. "But I don't mean identity in that sense."

"What do you mean then?" asked Shambhavi.

"I mean that when we are a spiritual student, our gender identity is omni-gender," said Merlyn. "It's no longer okay to develop the traditional qualities of one of the genders and forget about the rest. We have to be as strong as we are sensitive, as intelligent as we are feeling, and as logical as we are creative. Underneath (or above) our birth gender, we include it all. I know that isn't a very romantic idea. Romance implies that we need to be completed by another of a certain gender, and if we handle it correctly, we'll supposedly get what we need. But when we are complete, then life, relationships, and romance become a whole different playing field."

Shambhavi looked like he wasn't quite ready to give up on the romance idea, and changed the direction of the conversation.

"If not female, then at least you are single."

Not wanting to discuss her supposed new boyfriend, Merlyn said, "It's the same. On the spiritual path, single or partnered, everyone is both. And neither. Remember how the Bible says, *They neither marry nor are given in marriage, but are like God's angels in Heaven.* We are omni-relationship-status as much as we are omni-gender."

The idea of *omni* was something that Amira had been speaking to Merlyn about in Ajna Temple. It helped Merlyn to expand her concepts of both gender and relationships. She didn't tell Shambhavi about Amira. She concluded that if Amira wanted to talk to anyone, then she was quite capable of arranging it herself. Anyway, it was probably more a matter of who was willing to hear Amira than who Amira was willing to talk to.

Merlyn guessed that Shambhavi, deep in thought, was pondering his own situation. He probably thought that although there were disadvantages to being partnered, there were more disadvantages to being single. What would be a new concept to him was being neither single nor married, or being both at the same time. He would have thought that it sounded like a world of trouble.

Merlyn wondered if he was changing his mind about the bungalow offer. Regardless, it seemed best for him to have some idea of what he was letting into his life in close proximity.

Shambhavi started walking towards Prana Hall for the morning yoga classes with Veronica.

After a few steps, he turned back and said, "We'll help you move at the end of the week."

CHAPTER 33
VERY SOON

The following day, in the Wurt Wurt Koort Tearooms:

"You will be much closer to Waldmeer and Wurt Wurt Koort," said Rybert when Merlyn told him about her impending move to Shambhavi and Veronica's bungalow.

Merlyn caught Tom's disapproving look out of the corner of her eye. He was doing a shift while Rybert had the morning off. Mind you, Rybert hadn't gone anywhere and was still fussing around the cafe until Merlyn made him sit down with her.

"Yes," said Merlyn, "and, on that note, I have something else to say."

"Yes?" said Rybert, who was listening attentively.

He was old enough and intuitive enough to know when something important was about to be said.

"Although I very much appreciate your offer to save me from the world of singleness," Merlyn started with a soft smile.

He knew what was coming, or so he thought.

"The thing is," continued Merlyn, "you love Amira. Not me."

That wasn't quite what Rybert expected. He couldn't deny it was true. He did love Faith-Amira.

"And so," said Merlyn with a maturity that Rybert hadn't seen before, "I think it is best that we graciously abandon our recent attempt to have a closer relationship."

Merlyn felt it wise not to say anything else, and Rybert didn't quite know what to say. There were many avenues he could go down. What was his love for Faith-Amira? What was he hoping to achieve in his offer of a relationship with Merlyn? Regardless, he knew Merlyn was right and appreciated her courage. He wondered if Merlyn's new maturity came from Guru Gadubanud's presence at Prana Community or from Amira talking to her in Ajna Temple. Whatever it was, he felt both relief and respect.

Standing up, he leaned over, put his hand on her head, and kissed her forehead.

As Merlyn left, she spotted Tom's decidedly suspicious and disapproving stare.

"Bye, Tom," she said. "See you soon."

Tom huffed off.

"Very soon," said Merlyn with an amused smirk.

CHAPTER 34
OUTSIDERS AND INSIDERS

A week later, in the Wurt Wurt Koort Tearooms:

"Hello, Mer-Mer," Tom called out happily as Merlyn walked into the cafe after her Waldmeer Warrior's dance class with Shambhavi. "Lover-boy isn't here today."

Clearly, Rybert has told Tom that he and I are no longer a couple, thought Merlyn. *Not that we ever really were.*

Tom's little Brussels Griffon, Hardy, scuffled over to Merlyn for a pat. He wasn't supposed to be in the front of the shop, but was so delightful to all the customers that his bed in the backroom mostly remained empty.

During a quieter moment, Tom came and sat next to Merlyn, best of friends again.

"How's Guru Gadu-*bad* going?" asked Tom.

Merlyn laughed and offered, "Guru Gadu-banud."

"Guru Gad-*about*," said Tom.

Merlyn rolled her eyes with amusement. Her expression became more thoughtful, and she said, "In the question-and-answer session last night, I asked the Guru about the spiritual significance of being gay." Before Tom could crack a joke, she added, "I want to talk about this."

"Okay, what did he say?" sighed Tom.

"He said there is no spiritual significance in it," said Merlyn.

"Was that it?" asked Tom.

"He also said that minority sexual preference groups are, by nature, small, but with the current climate, the groups are growing beyond their natural limits."

"What does that mean?" asked Tom defensively.

"I guess," said Merlyn, "it is part of the swing into a more balanced world."

"We can use the numbers," said Tom.

"He did say that being gay shouldn't become the God instead of what really matters in life."

"It matters to me," said Tom tartly.

"And it matters to me, too," said Merlyn. "I'm not an outsider, Tom, because I see the inside of you. You're not just some amusing gay entertainment. You're an intelligent, beautiful being."

MANDALA'S END

CHAPTER 35
FORTY DAYS

I n *Prana Community:*

It was the end of the forty-day mandala, which began at Mahashivratri. It was also the last day that Guru Gadubanud was at Prana Community.

Most mornings, Merlyn had been travelling to Prana, from Shambhavi and Veronica's property, to do Veronica's yoga class (even though it wasn't her favourite). She did it out of respect for living in their bungalow and for Shambhavi (who *was* her favourite).

Being the end of the mandala, the yellow threads tied around everyone's wrists were to be removed. They had been worn as a reminder to integrate the five elements of earth, water, wind, fire, and space into the body to facilitate health and vibrancy.

Mandalas are based on the idea that anything done consecutively for forty days makes an imprint on the body as a habit. Our bodies' physiology changes every forty to forty-eight days, giving us raw material to work with.

After Guru Gadubanud's final talk, the threads would be

untied and tied onto a tree branch or dug into the earth. It would be a ceremonial process done by each person privately.

Merlyn joined the line at Ajna Temple that evening, ready for the foot washing station and the acupuncture hallway, which helped to awaken the body through the pressure points.

For a moment, she panicked when she realised that the woman in front of her with long, dark, curly hair was Esther. However, seeing as there was no Ben, she relaxed somewhat and decided to make the most of the opportunity.

"I didn't realise you were here," said Merlyn with as much goodwill as she could muster.

It was a black evening with no moonlight. The temple did not have exterior lighting because the small hydroelectric generator was reserved for the interior lighting. Merlyn could not easily see Esther's expression. However, she felt her energy was less guarded and hostile, and more approachable.

"I'm having some time off work," said Esther, "and have been here for the past week."

That's a surprise, thought Merlyn. *I haven't seen her. And it's surprising that Esther would take time from her work. She is very tied up with her profession as a psychologist.*

"I haven't seen you around," said Merlyn.

"No, I've been keeping to myself," said Esther. "They put me in your old room."

"Did they tell you it was my room?" asked Merlyn.

"No," said Esther, "I could just tell."

CHAPTER 36
CAUTION TO THE WIND

Once inside Ajna Temple, Merlyn could have smoothly parted company with Esther and sat at another point of the circular room. However, she chose not to. As usual, Guru Gadubanud gave an insightful and motivating talk.

Merlyn and Esther sat there together, and Merlyn felt the ice melting between them. She also felt that she may never know what happened between Ben and Esther, and that it may not be hers to know. There was no denying the sense of betrayal from Esther, as a therapist, fellow member of Prana, woman, and friend.

Was it really betrayal? Merlyn thought. *If someone else's actions betray our sensitivities, is it a betrayal? Or is it that the person is simply doing what they want, what they perceive as in the best interests of their happiness? Just because something hurts us, does it mean we are betrayed? Maybe, they are just living their lives.*

Merlyn told herself that when she removed her Mahashivratri wrist thread, she would consciously remove any resentment towards Esther. Esther would be free, and Ben would be free, at least in Merlyn's mind. She would be free of the burden of remembering it.

"One day, it will not be necessary for you to do any of these processes," said Guru Gadubanud in conclusion. "You won't need to do spiritual practices because you will have become the very thing that you have practised for years. You will look at the elements and not see them as outside of you. You will look at the master and not see him as someone other than you. You will look at those you love and see them as part of your life fibre."

Touching the yellow thread of the nearest person to him, the guru continued, "The Abhaya Sutra (the thread) has been a reminder to integrate the elements into yourself. After forty days, it has become a part of you. Even if you forget, your body will still remember. That is why, when we are close to someone in a physical way for an extended period, our actual body will grieve if they are no longer available to us. Our body has its own memory."

Guru Gadubanud moved around the temple, blessing each person, and said, "These spiritual processes and practices help to transform your being on all the various levels. So, do them diligently, and you will reap the rewards. It is my wish and blessing that you have benefited from my presence. Be assured that I will be with you whenever you need my assistance."

No one clapped because you don't clap in temples. It made the sense of appreciation even more profound and poignant.

As he left the temple, Guru Gadubanud said, "One of your members has decided to return with me to the ashram in Southern India."

There was a collective gasp, and everyone looked around to see who would have made such a commitment. Then all eyes turned in Merlyn's direction as the guru pointed her way.

Merlyn knew it wasn't her, so she looked at Esther, who smiled and acknowledged the guru with namaste hands to her forehead. It was her.

Later that evening, before beginning the forty-five-minute drive back to the bungalow, Merlyn stood alone on the cliff's edge outside Ajna Temple. Her eyes had become accustomed to the dark, and she could see well enough to be safe.

Standing next to the tree that was to be the recipient of her thread, she lifted the faded yellow piece of yarn as high as possible. The wind picked up around her. She let the wind grab it.

Higher and higher, the thread flew like a reckless dancer, throwing caution to the wind, no longer aware of the prepared choreography.

Higher and higher, until it was a tiny piece of nothing in a vast sky of everything destined for God only knows where.

If God knows where, thought Merlyn, *then there can be no safer journey.*

SUMMARY OF WALDMEER SERIES

A multi-generational journey of spiritual awakening, healing, and the spaces between worlds.

Beneath the surface of an idyllic coastal village, unseen forces stir. Waldmeer is a place where the visible and invisible meet—where inter-dimensional realms brush against everyday life, and where emotional truths rise quietly but undeniably.

Told across seven books, the *Waldmeer Series* follows Maria–Amira from the groundedness of her rural home to the doorways into higher realms of perception and spiritual transformation. Around her, those she loves and seeks to help are drawn into their own awakenings, resistances, and reckonings.

Waldmeer moves between ordinary moments and otherworldly initiations. Between earthly love and higher love. Between who we think we are... and what we truly are.

At times tender, at times confronting, these stories unfold in layers—personal, relational, and metaphysical.

ABOUT THE AUTHOR

On the beach at Lorne, Australia (the coastal village Waldmeer is based on).

Donna Goddard is a spiritual author whose work blends clarity, devotion, and metaphysical insight. With 25+ published books across spiritual nonfiction, fiction, poetry, and children's literature, she writes to uplift consciousness and offer healing through words.

Donna's Facebook author page has over 400,000 followers worldwide, and her YouTube channel has received 4 million views. Her books are read by spiritual seekers globally and are known for their honesty, poetic style, and transformative energy.

Her writing is an offering—to help others awaken their own inner spirit, trust its guidance, and create a life of depth, beauty, and quiet joy.

All links at https://linktr.ee/donnagoddard

Ratings and Reviews

Donna would be grateful for any ratings or reviews.

ALSO BY DONNA GODDARD

Fiction

Waldmeer Series: A Spiritual Fiction Series
Nanima Series: Spiritual Fiction
Enanika Series: Visionary Fiction
Riverland Series (children's fiction 6 to 9 years)
Foxie (children's fiction 7 to 12 years)

Nonfiction

Love and Devotion Series
Sweet Spirit Series
Consciousness Series
Being Meditation Series
Many Moments Series
Poetry Series
Love's Longing
Dance: A Spiritual Affair
Writing: A Spiritual Voice

www.ingramcontent.com/pod-product-compliance
Lightning Source LLC
Chambersburg PA
CBHW020527120726
47904CB00003B/991